Barkus

The Most Fun

BOOK 3

BY PATRICIA MACLACHLAN · ILLUSTRATED BY MARC BOUTAVANT

chronicle books · san francisco

For two very smart rescue dog friends of mine—
Teddy and Annie. —PM

Library of Congress Cataloging-in-Publication Data available.

ISBN 978-1-4521-7334-4

Manufactured in China.

Design by Sara Gillingham Studio.
Typeset in Harriet and Lunchbox.

10 9 8 7 6 5 4 3 2 1

Chronicle Books LLC
680 Second Street, San Francisco, California 94107
Chronicle Books—we see things differently. Become part of our community at www.chroniclekids.com.

CONTENTS

WHAT BARKUS KNOWS 2

THE CRAZY COWS OF SPRING 14

THE MOST FUN! 28

A WINTER'S TALE 38

WHAT BARKUS KNOWS

Barkus is excited.

He knows something.

Barkus *always* knows something.

My father puts a grill in the car.

Barkus knows all about grills.

Grills mean hamburgers,
hot dogs, sausages.

My mother puts tents
and sleeping bags in the car.

Barkus knows all about
sleeping bags and tents.

CAMPING!

"There's a tent for you and Barkus and one for your father and me," says my mother.

"What about Baby?" I ask.

Barkus's ears go up.

"Camping is not for cats," says my mother. "Miss Daley will take care of Baby."

Barkus jumps up in the way back of the car. He likes to look out the back window and wag his tail when we pass cars. Sometimes people wave at Barkus.

I climb into the back seat with my fishing pole and three books to read if it rains.

I wave at Miss Daley as we drive away.

“Are you all right in the back?” I call to Barkus.

“Woof.”

I know the sound of that Barkus woof.

He knows something.

Barkus has a secret.

When we get to our campsite, my mother opens the back door of the car.

Barkus jumps out.

Baby jumps down behind him!

That was Barkus's secret!

“Oh no, camping is not for cats!” repeats my mother.

But when we put up the first tent, Baby runs inside.

“Baby likes camping!” I say. “See?”

“I see,” says my mother. “But she won’t like the water. Water is not for cats.”

Barkus rolls in the sand. Sand flies everywhere, like rain.

Baby runs to the water. She jumps over little waves, shaking the water from her feet.

“I think Baby likes the water, too,” I say.

“Hmm,” says my mother. “Baby will NOT like nighttime when the owls screech in the trees.”

But that night inside our tent, Barkus snores.

I watch Baby.

Baby sits in the tent screen opening, listening to the calls of owls.

And she watches the moon rise over the water.

Then Baby sleeps.

The next day I do not catch a fish. Barkus runs with Baby, who finds something to chase. My father grills sausages.

The day goes by too quickly.

The car is packed up to go home again.

The drive is long.

"How are things back there?" asks my father, looking at me in the rearview mirror.

I answer with one of my father's expressions.

"As expected," I call to him.

"How are things back there, Barkus?" I ask.

"Woof."

It is a contented woof.

I peer through the sleeping bags and tents in the way back.

There is Barkus.

There is Baby. All curled up.

THE CRAZY COWS OF SPRING

Barkus stands by our car.

"Woof!"

He knows that every spring we visit my grandparents' farm in the hills.

When my father opens the way back to put in suitcases, Barkus jumps right in.

"Smartest dog in the whole world," my father says.

Baby jumps right in, too.

"Smartest cat, too," I say.

JAN California 2017
BRK3NB1
dmv.ca.gov

We drive past many farms. Barkus wags his tail at cows in the meadows. He woofs at horses.

Then I see it—the road to my grandfather Jess's farm.

Grandfather Jess waves to us from the barn door. Barkus races up to him. Jess hugs Barkus.

He hugs me.

The cows come out into the sunlight.

I know them by name: Jane, with a star on her face, Flora, Nora, Dora, and Emmy, the calf.

Then it happens.

Maybe it is a sudden sweet breeze.

The cows kick up their heels.

They race around the meadow.

They run over to the fence and push through, splintering the top rail.

“Hey,” yells Jess. “Stop!”

Grandmother Bett runs out of the house and waves.

“It’s spring, Jess!” she calls.

The cows trot onto the main road. Barkus and I cut across the field to head them off. Baby follows.

The cows slow down when they see Barkus in the front.

The cows pass the small pond. Two ducks watch.

The horses in the meadow look up, surprised.

The cows go down South Street headed to the village.

Cars stop so the cows can pass. The cows pass the school. They pass the post office.

Barkus leads them around the library, twice! Green spring grass is growing there and the cows are happy.

Then the cows are tired.

"Woof!" Barkus walks toward the road.

The cows follow Barkus back up South Street.

The cows walk over the Stone River Bridge.

They pass the small pond.

They turn onto the farm road to their meadow.

I hold the paddock door open for them.

Jess feeds them grain to thank them for coming home.

"Happy spring," Jess says to the cows.

"Woof," says Barkus.

Barkus is tired. He's worked hard. But that night Barkus won't come inside to sleep. He stays out in the field.

"He'll keep Dora company," says Jess, turning off the porch light.

The next morning, I hear Barkus.

"Woof. Woof! Woof!"

Barkus knows something!

I hear Jess go out the door.

Baby and I go out to see what Barkus knows.

“Dora has a calf!” says Jess happily.

Barkus woofs softly, as if telling us “hush.”

“It’s a girl,” says Jess. “Guess what Barkus and I have named her.”

“What?” I ask.

“Spring!” says Jess.

“Woof!” says Barkus.

And then Barkus lies down in the spring grass and goes to sleep.

THE MOST FUN!

Barkus loves fall. He rolls in the neat piles of raked leaves, jumping out at Baby.

I love fall because I love the parade!

"Woof," says Barkus.

Barkus knows.

The Ambling of the Calves Parade celebrates all the animals people love. There is a band and baton twirlers and floats. Once I rode on one dressed as a red leaf.

"We can't take Baby!" says my father. "You have to have leashes for the animals you take to the parade."

“I bought a small cat leash for Baby,” says my mother.

“What?” asks my father.

My mother slips the red leash around Baby’s neck. She twists and escapes.

My father and I laugh.

Barkus waits by the car.

Baby jumps on Barkus's back and up into the car.

"Smartest dog," says my father.

"Smartest cat," I add.

The parade begins with the horses and their lively colts.

A band goes by. Children pull wagons of caged chickens, some roosters with colorful red combs, and some Silkies, white and fluffy.

The llamas walk by with their graceful necks. One comes over to touch noses with Barkus.

Two large floats pass by, both filled with dogs. The first has GOOD DOGS painted on a banner.

The second has a banner that says SORT OF GOOD DOGS, making people laugh and clap.

Barkus barks at them all.

"Woof. Woof!"

The dogs answer back in a din of barking.

And then, finally come the calves, wearing wreaths of flowers around their necks.

Barkus pulls his leash out of my father's hand and prances next to the band! Baby gets on Barkus's back.

The crowd cheers!

And that is how a photographer takes a picture of Barkus and Baby.

The picture is in the town newspaper the next day.

Beneath the picture is written:

“Barkus and Friends—the Most Fun!”

True, they did have fun.

But I had the most fun of all!

A WINTER'S TALE

Snowflakes fall as we pack to drive to our cabin.

The skis and ski poles are on the car roof. Warm sleeping bags and pillows are in the way back.

Barkus jumps right in.

"Smartest dog," says my father.

Baby jumps right in.

"Smartest cat," I add.

The snow falls a little harder as we drive. It begins to stick on the road.

The wind begins to blow. There are no other cars on the road.

Barkus sighs. He is bored.

He flops down and goes to sleep.

As we get closer to our cabin the wind shakes the car.

My father has to drive around some tree branches that have been blown down.

Soon we see the hill that leads to the cabin.

"We'll be there just in time. This will be a big storm," says my father.

When my father stops the car, Barkus jumps down into a drift of snow. I carry Baby tucked in my jacket.

"Let's go in and start a fire," says my father.

"Woof," agrees Barkus.

The house is cold. No electricity. No heat.

There are stacks of wood by the fireplace.

"Woof."

Barkus knows.

My father builds a fire. It sends light across the walls of the cabin.

We put down the sleeping bags and pillows in front of the fire. My mother finds oil lamps and candles. It will be dark soon.

“Too stormy for skiing,” says my mother.

“But what will we do?!” I ask.

“You can read one or two or three of your many books,” says my father.

“We’ll get out a huge jigsaw puzzle and we’ll eat delicious food,” says my mother.

“Woof,” says Barkus.

“We can’t grill out in this wind and snow,” says my father.

“I made lots of grilled chicken and biscuits,” says my mother. “And I brought frozen corncobs from summer. We’ll warm them over the fire.”

Barkus woofs at the fireplace. My father puts more wood on the fire.

"And then, when it is dark, we'll do what your grandfather Jess always did on stormy nights," says my mother.

"What?" I ask.

"He told stories," says my mother. "Stories about when he was young."

"I'm young now," I say. "I don't have any stories."

"We'll make up a story after dinner," says my mother. "What will we call it?"

" 'A Winter's Tale,' " says my father.

"The story will be about us," I say. "And Barkus and Baby."

"Of course," says my mother.

We have dinner. Baby eats her own food. Barkus eats his food and three homemade biscuits, hiding another one in a sleeping bag for later.

Outside, the wind blows small branches against the roof. My mother brings out some quilts. My father makes hot cocoa.

It is time for the story.

“A Winter’s Tale,” begins my father.

Barkus thumps his tail against the floor.

“Not that tail,” says my father.

"Once, on a stormy night, a family cuddled in front of a roaring fire," says my father.

"Woof."

"Barkus knows
he is family,"
I say. "And Baby, too."

"Baby came to them
on fairy wings,"
says my mother.

"That's not true!" I say.

"It's a story, Nicky.
Anything can be true in a
story," says my mother.

"The dog, Barkus, was a master fire builder," says my father. "He kept the family warm."

"Woof."

"The cat, Baby, had brought her pen and paper. She was writing a poem about winter," I say.

"What was the poem?" asks my mother.

I think for a moment.

"Winter cold
and sparkling white—
blowing wind
all through the night."

“Baby wrote that?” asks my father.

“She is a published poet,” I say. “And it’s a story. Anything can be true.”

“The family slept all through the night, except Barkus, who tended the fire.”

I yawn.

My mother blows out the oil lamp and pulls her sleeping bag around her.

Barkus yawns his squeaky dog yawn.

“How does this story end?” I ask yawning, too.

"The family lived happily ever after," says my father. "As expected."

"Woof." Barkus's woof is soft and sleepy.

My eyes close.

"As expected," I say.